The Raccoon and the Bee Tree

The Raccoon and the Bee Tree

—

by Charles A. Eastman
and Elaine Goodale Eastman

—

Illustrated by Susan Turnbull

—

A Prairie Tale

SOUTH DAKOTA STATE HISTORICAL SOCIETY PRESS

PIERRE

A PRAIRIE TALE FROM THE
SOUTH DAKOTA STATE HISTORICAL SOCIETY PRESS

Editor: Nancy Tystad Koupal • Introduction: Martyn Beeny
Designer: Mark Conahan • Production: Patti Edman

The Raccoon and the Bee Tree is Volume 4 in the Prairie Tale Series.

This publication is funded, in part, by
the Great Plains Education Foundation, Inc., Aberdeen, S.Dak.

Library of Congress Cataloging-in-Publication Data
Eastman, Charles Alexander, 1858-1939.
The raccoon and the bee tree / by Charles A. Eastman and Elaine Goodale
Eastman ; illustrated by Susan Turnbull.
p. cm. -- (Prairie tale series ; v. 4)
I S B N 978-0-9798940-8-4
1 . Indians of North America--Great Plains--Folklore. I . Eastman, Elaine
Goodale, 1863-1953. II . Turnbull, Susan. III . Title.

E78.G73E27 2009

398.2089 97078--DC22

2008050512
Printed in Canada
13 12 11 10 09 1 2 3 4 5

Introduction

THE RACCOON AND THE BEE TREE is a traditional
American Indian tale. The story takes place in the prairie
woodlands of eastern South Dakota or western Minnesota.
While much of South Dakota has few trees, some parts along
the rivers are quite woody. Although the woodlands are usually
small, they are home to many creatures. Raccoons look for food,
birds build nests, squirrels search for acorns, and bees make honey
in the trees. Long ago, when this story was first told, bears also
lived all over this region. Now, you are unlikely to find bears
anywhere in South Dakota except the Black Hills.

There are no humans in this story, but the animals act in ways
that might be human. Both American Indian and European
stories often use animals to represent humans and teach lessons.
In *The Raccoon and the Bee Tree*, the main character is a raccoon.

He is adventurous and curious. He ends up in trouble because he takes something that is not his. It is a lesson that everyone should learn.

Author Charles Eastman, whose Indian name was Ohiyesa, learned these lessons growing up in southwestern Minnesota and Canada. He was a Wahpeton Dakota (Santee Sioux), and his family taught him the traditional ways of his people. He listened to tales just like *The Raccoon and the Bee Tree*. When he was a teenager, he moved to Flandreau in Dakota Territory. At his new school, he often read European fables. Fables contain a moral or message, just as many American Indian stories do.

When he grew up, Charles Eastman became a doctor and worked on the Pine Ridge Indian Reservation in western South Dakota. There he met Elaine Goodale, a white woman from Massachusetts. They married in 1891. Charles Eastman often told his own children the old stories that he had learned at campfires and gatherings when he was a child. These stories were not written down. People had to listen carefully and remember all the details so that they could tell them to others later. *The Raccoon and the Bee Tree* was one of these special campfire stories.

Elaine told Charles that he should write down this story and all the others he could remember. When he wrote them down, he combined the traditional American Indian story with the style of the fables he had learned. He included a moral at the end. Elaine Eastman edited the tales to make them easier to read. Together, the Eastmans first published *The Raccoon and the Bee Tree* in a book called *Wigwam Evenings* in 1909.

THE RACCOON HAD been asleep all day in the snug
hollow of a tree. The dusk was coming on when he awoke,
stretched himself once or twice, and jumping down from
the top of the tall, dead stump in which he made his home, set
out to look for his supper.

In the midst of the woods there was a lake, and all along the lake shore there rang out the alarm cries of the water people as the Raccoon came nearer and nearer.

First the Swan gave a scream of warning. The Crane repeated the cry, and from the very middle of the lake the Loon, swimming low, took it up and echoed it back over the still water.

The Raccoon sped merrily on, and finding no unwary bird that he could seize, he picked up a few mussel-shells from the beach, cracked them neatly and ate the sweet meat.

5

A little further on, as he was leaping hither and thither through the long, tangled meadow grass, he landed with all four feet on a family of Skunks—father, mother, and twelve little ones, who were curled up sound asleep in a soft bed of broken dry grass.

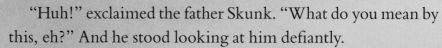

"Huh!" exclaimed the father Skunk. "What do you mean by this, eh?" And he stood looking at him defiantly.

"Oh, excuse me, excuse me," begged the Raccoon. "I am very sorry. I did not mean to do it! I was just running along and I did not see you at all."

"Better be careful where you step next time," grumbled the Skunk, and the Raccoon was glad to hurry on.

Running up a tall tree he came upon two red Squirrels in one nest, but before he could get his paws upon one of them they were scolding angrily from the topmost bough.

"Come down, friends!" called the Raccoon. "What are you doing up there? Why, I wouldn't harm you for anything!"

"Ugh, you can't fool us," chattered the Squirrels, and the Raccoon went on.

Deep in the woods, at last, he found a great hollow tree which attracted him by a peculiar sweet smell.

He sniffed and sniffed, and went round and round till he saw something trickling down a narrow crevice.

He tasted it and it was deliciously sweet.

He ran up the tree and down again, and at last found an opening into which he could thrust his paw.

He brought it out covered with honey!

Now the Raccoon was happy. He ate and scooped, and scooped and ate the golden, trickling honey with both forepaws until his pretty, pointed face was daubed all over.

Suddenly he tried to get a paw into his ear. Something hurt him terribly just then,

and the next minute his sensitive nose was frightfully stung. He rubbed his face with both sticky paws. The sharp stings came thicker and faster, and he wildly clawed the air. At last he forgot to hold on to the branch any longer, and with a screech he tumbled to the ground.

There he rolled and rolled on the dead leaves till he was covered with leaves from head to foot, for they stuck to his fine, sticky fur, and most of all they covered his eyes and his striped face.

Mad with fright and pain he dashed through the forest calling to some one of his own kind to come to his aid.

The moon was now bright, and many of the woods people were abroad. A second Raccoon heard the call and went to meet it.

But when he saw a frightful object plastered with dry leaves racing madly toward him he turned and ran for his life, for he did not know what this thing might be.

The Raccoon who had been stealing the honey ran after him as fast as he could, hoping to overtake and beg the other to help him get rid of his leaves.

So they ran and they ran out of the woods on to the shining white beach around the lake. Here a Fox met them, but after one look at the queer object, which was chasing the frightened Raccoon he too turned and ran at his best speed.

Presently a young Bear came loping out of the wood and sat up on his haunches to see them go by. But when he got a good look at the Raccoon who was plastered with dead leaves, he scrambled up a tree to be out of the way.

By this time the poor Raccoon was so frantic that he scarcely knew what he was doing. He ran up the tree after the Bear and got hold of his tail.

"Woo, woo!" snarled the Bear, and the Raccoon let go.

He was tired out and dreadfully ashamed. He did now what he ought to have done at the very first—he jumped into the lake and washed off most of the leaves.

Then he got back to his hollow tree and curled himself up and licked and licked his soft fur till he had licked himself clean, and then he went to sleep.

The midnight hunter steals at his own risk.

Word list

abroad – out of doors
bough – a large branch of a tree
crevice – a crack forming an opening
daubed – covered; painted
defiantly – boldly resistant
delicacy – a rare and special food
demure – shy; modest
feasting – eating lots of good food
frantic – desperate with pain and fear
haunches – the top of the leg and backside
hither and thither – here and there
loping – running in a long, loose, jumping manner
midst – in the middle of
ought – should
queer – strange
range – arrange; take up a position
scarcely – hardly; not quite
scholars – students
scolding – telling off
snug – comfortable; cozy
thrust – shove; push hard
troublesome – causing trouble
unwary – not cautious or watchful

Bibliography

Badt, Karen Luisa. *Charles Eastman: Sioux Physician and Author.* New York: Chelsea House Publishers, 1995.

Copeland, Marion W. *Charles Alexander Eastman (Ohiyesa).* Boise, Idaho: Boise State University, 1978.

Eastman, Charles A. *From the Deep Woods to Civilization: Chapters in the Autobiography of an Indian.* Boston: Little, Brown & Co., 1916.

Eastman, Charles A. *Indian Boyhood.* Greenwich, Conn.: Fawcett Publications, 1972.

Eastman, Charles A. *Red Hunters and the Animal People.* New York: Harper & Brothers, 1904.

Eastman, Charles A., and Elaine Goodale Eastman. *Wigwam Evenings: Sioux Folk Tales Retold.* Boston: Little, Brown & Co., 1909.

Graber, Kay, ed. *Sister to the Sioux: The Memoirs of Elaine Goodale Eastman, 1885–91.* Lincoln, Nebr.: University of Nebraska Press, 1978.

Lee, Betsy. *Charles Eastman: The Story of an American Indian.* Minneapolis: Dillon Press, 1979.

Sargent, Theodore D. *The Life of Elaine Goodale Eastman.* Lincoln, Nebr.: University of Nebraska Press, 2005.

Wilson, Raymond. *Ohiyesa: Charles Eastman, Santee Sioux.* Chicago: University of Illinois Press, 1983.